The Adventures of Harriet Hamster

Written by
Nancy Springs Morris

Illustrated by
Yhonny Sanoja

MYND MATTERS

Copyright © 2022 by Nancy Springs Morris.

All rights reserved. This book is a work of fiction. Names, characters, and incidents either are products of the author's imagination or are used fictitiously.

No part of this book may be reproduced in any written, electronic, or recorded form or photocopied without written permission from the publisher or author. If you would like permission to use material from the book (other than for review purposes), please contact the author or publisher. Thank you for your support of the author's rights.

To purchase books in bulk or for additional information, contact Mynd Matters Publishing
715 Peachtree Street NE
Suites 100 & 200
Atlanta, GA 30308
www.myndmatterspublishing.com

978-1-957092-48-5 (pbk)
978-1-957092-49-2 (hdcv)

FIRST EDITION

To my two beautiful daughters who, as little girls, were surrounded by, and read, books of all kinds. (They had a hamster named Theus who escaped from his cage while they were visiting their beloved grandmother in Charlotte, North Carolina.)

To my beloved grandson Victor, who, too, is surrounded by books of all kinds. (He has a dog named Monte Fishstick and a turtle named Miss Tippy Toes.)

To my beloved husband, Lloyd Belton Morris, who actually transported the real Harriet Hamster to Myrtle Beach, South Carolina and participated in the World Amateur Handicap Golf Tournament.

It was the last day of school and Mrs. Sinclair was excited to go home and do whatever she pleased. She looked over at the nearby glass tank and smiled. Harriet, the class pet, was also going home with Mrs. Sinclair and she was thrilled.

Happy Retirement, Mrs. Sinclair and Harriet! was printed on the chalkboard in big letters.

Some of the children brought gifts of flowers, candy, note cards, a puzzle book or two, and colored pens. There was a plastic maze tube and a package of sunflower seeds for Harriet.

"Will you write to us, Mrs. Sinclair?" whispered Jackie.

"Of course I will," she replied.

"I'll send you postcards with smiling faces."

"Good-bye, Mrs. Sinclair! Good-bye, Harriet!" yelled the children as the bell rang for dismissal and they filed out of the classroom.

The next morning, Mrs. Sinclair turned over to smell sizzling bacon, brewed black coffee, and home-baked cinnamon buns.

"Who is creating those wonderful smells?" she wondered aloud. "Oh my! It's my first day at home since I retired. How sweet of Mr. Sinclair to make breakfast."

Mrs. Sinclair made her way to the nearby glass tank and gathered Harriet before heading to the kitchen.

With a broad smile, Mr. Sinclair poured his wife a cup of coffee and offered sugar and cream.

"Have you looked at the calendar?" asked Mr. Sinclair. "The World Amateur Handicap Golf Tournament is scheduled in three days."

"Yes dear, but what shall we do with Harriet?"

"We can get a sitter. Maybe the young boy up the street since he enjoys pet sitting."

Mrs. Sinclair smiled from ear-to-ear.
"Marvelous idea!" she said.

Mr. and Mrs. Sinclair got an early start the next morning. Mr. Sinclair placed their suitcases near the door and Mrs. Sinclair went into the family room to tell Harriet that she would be left with a pet sitter while they were away.

As Mrs. Sinclair rubbed Harriet's fur and told her about the sitter, she remembered the snacks on the kitchen counter.
She had to pack them for their trip.
She quickly put Harriet back inside the glass tank and headed toward the kitchen without closing the lid.

Harriet really wanted to go on the trip with Mr. and Mrs. Sinclair.
She looked back and forth trying to decide what to do.
As she heard footsteps approaching, she quickly scurried out of the glass tank and snuck into Mr. Sinclair's golf bag.

It was a lovely day for the drive to Myrtle Beach, South Carolina. For Harriet, it was a bumpy ride but within no time, she fell asleep at the bottom of the golf bag. Mrs. Sinclair had plans to rest, enjoy the beach, read a good book, and shop. Mr. Sinclair just wanted to place big in the tournament.

The next morning, Mr. Sinclair was up early to tee off at eight o'clock, and so was Harriet! Mr. Sinclair put his golf bag down on the first tee box because there was a long delay.

Seeing a chance for freedom, Harriet jumped onto the tee box before darting into the woods. Once she slowed down, Harriet surveyed the place where she found herself. It was very different from Mr. and Mrs. Sinclair's home and the classroom at school.

After a few minutes of looking around, Harriet could find nothing at all to do.

Staring into the eyes of a grasshopper,
Harriet said boldly, "Are you bored?"
"Never," said the grasshopper while leaping
high off the ground and over her head.
I amuse myself while I exercise.
Ask Gray Squirrel."

14

Harriet scampered farther into the woods.
A chattering noise came from nearby.
It was Gray Squirrel cracking an acorn.

"Pardon me," said Harriet.
"Are you bored?"
"Not the least bit," said Gray Squirrel.
"I gnaw and chew to keep my front
teeth strong and sharp. Ask Firefly."

Harriet stopped to think of her life with Mrs. Sinclair.
"I do miss those little belly rubs and
the good food I've enjoyed," she thought.
Distracted by the flicker of a light,
she ran after it in hopes of being led to Mr. Sinclair.

Only, following the light took her deeper into the woods.
When the light perched on some tall grass to rest,
she asked, "Are you bored?"
"Never," said Firefly.
"I use my luminescence (lu-mi-nes-cence)
to protect myself from danger."

Poor Harriet began to shiver with fear as she tried to remember how to get back onto the green.

"Run for your life!" squealed a very large rat. "Run for your life!" She watched from afar as a slithering snake flickered its tongue in and out to track down food.

Harriet came to a halt as beads of sweat gathered on her forehead and then dripped to the ground. She panted for air.

Suddenly, she felt a shadow towering over her small body. As she looked up, what she thought was a tree trunk moved slightly, showing a pair of ears, whiskers, and a long tail.

"My child, call me Grandmother Rat. You are so lucky! Thank goodness that snake went in the other direction."

"I'm Harriet," she replied, shaking nervously.

"Hey! We look alike, except your tail is longer. Are we related?"

"Yes, I am a rodent just like you but of a different breed," replied Grandmother Rat. Harriet looked at Grandmother Rat and asked the same question she had asked all of the animals in the wild. "Are you bored?"

"Not the least bit. I live in large groups called colonies. Sometimes we go near the water, on garbage dumps and in old buildings, and even in people's homes. My life is exciting!"

"I want to go home!" cried Harriet.
"This is not my way of living."
"Follow me and I will get you out of the wild."
Grandmother Rat looked at Harriet knowingly.

Arriving near the edge of the woods, Grandmother Rat
stayed out of sight as she nudged Harriet onto the green.
Harried buried herself under a leaf and waited
for her chance to sneak into the golf bag once again.

"Return to your world, Harriet. You have good food,
shelter from cold and rain, and you are safe.
But, most importantly, you are loved," said Grandmother Rat.

Mr. Sinclair's bag tumbled over onto its side.
Harriet's chance had come!
She ran quickly and landed head first
at the bottom of the warm bag. Harriet sighed with relief.
It was time to go back home with Mr. and Mrs. Sinclair.

COME BACK SOON

THE END

25

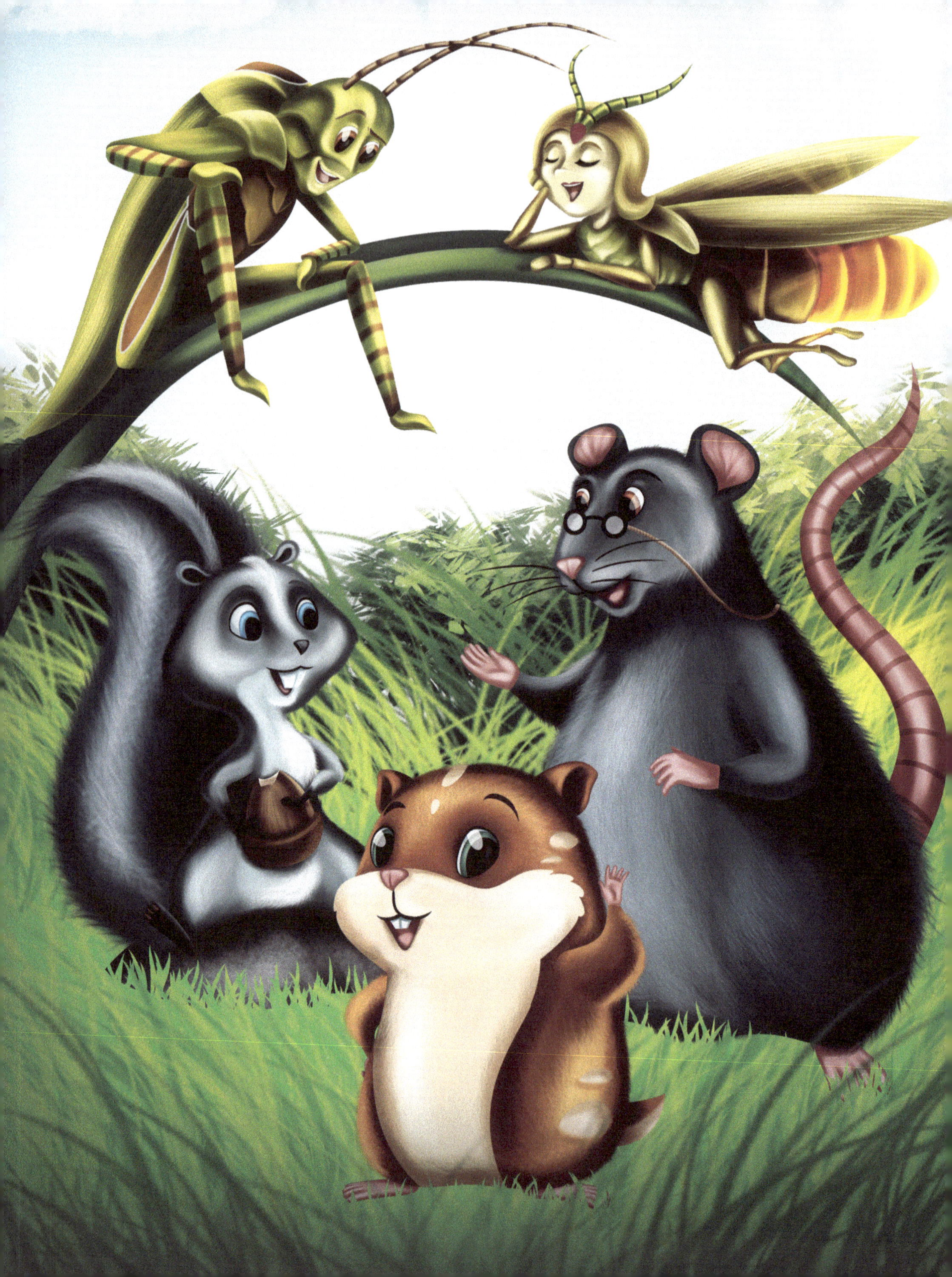

Printed in the USA
CPSIA information can be obtained
at www.ICGtesting.com
JSHW071911090923
48140JS00011B/77

9 781957 092485